First Little Readers™ E

Ladybug's Birthday

by Liza Charlesworth

ISBN: 978-1-338-29786-7

Illustrated by Tammie Lyon

First printing, June 2018.

Ladybug woke up and smiled.
"Today is my birthday," she said.
"I can't wait to play with my pals."

Ladybug saw Grasshopper.
"Today is my birthday!" she said.
"Can you play?"

"Sorry," said Grasshopper.
"I need to go meet some pals."
Hop, hop, hop!

Ladybug saw Worm.
"Today is my birthday!" she said.
"Can you play?"

"Sorry," said Worm.
"I need to go meet some pals."
Wiggle, wiggle, wiggle!

Ladybug saw Butterfly.
"Today is my birthday!" she said.
"Can you play?"

"Sorry," said Butterfly.
"I need to go meet some pals."
Flutter, flutter, flutter!

Ladybug saw Snail.
"Today is my birthday!" she said.
"Can you play?"

"Sorry," said Snail.
"I need to go meet some pals."
Slide, slide, slide!

"Boo-hoo!," cried Ladybug.
"Nobody will play,
so I will go to the garden."

Creep, creep, creep.
Cry, cry, cry.

Hey!
In the garden she saw Grasshopper and Worm and Butterfly and Snail.

"SURPRISE!" yelled the pals. "Happy birthday to you!"

The pals had a cake with candles.
"Oh, my!" said Ladybug.

"Make a wish!" yelled Grasshopper and Worm and Butterfly and Snail. Then Ladybug said, "I wish everyone had great pals like you."